The Silence
Of
JACOB SWAIN

Previously Published

Up In Irish Brooklyn
Not a drop to drink. . .
Belle of the Ball
Spying on You
Unveiled Echoes
The Smoking Contest
Sweet, Sauer, and Sad
Welcome Sundays
The Sensation
A Jack is a King

The Silence *Of* JACOB SWAIN

Let me live unseen, unknown
Thus unlamented let me die
Steal from the world
And not a stone tell where I lie.
Solitude by Alexander Pope
Early 18th Century, in public domain

NORMAN KEIFETZ

ISBN: 978-1-64945-375-4   (Paperback Edition)
ISBN: 978-1-64945-376-1   (Hardcover Edition)
ISBN: 978-1-64945-380-8   (E-book Edition)

Some characters and events in this book are fictitious. Any similarity to real persons, living or dead, is coincidental and not intended by the author.

Any people depicted in stock imagery provided by Pexel are models, and such images are being used for illustrative purposes only.
Certain stock imagery © Pexel.

Book Ordering Information

Phone Number: 347-901-4929 or 347-901-4920
Email: info@globalsummithouse.com
Global Summit House
www.globalsummithouse.com

Printed in the United States of America

DEDICATION

**For all those who were forced
to face the gruesome inhumanity.**

Very few were surprised when the 20-year old pitcher, Jake Swain, rose from the lowly Delmarva Ponies in the A- Half Season League in the Baltimore organization all the way up to the Norfolk Seagulls in Triple A, International League, by-passing minor league assignments in Frederick and Bowie. The kid already had a devastating fastball along with a sinker, and a devilish curve and screwball. Impossible to find that in a player so young and inexperienced. But believe or not the kid was being compared to the best pitchers in history, the likes of Sandy Koufax, Bob Gibson, Juan Marichal and Whitey Ford and he hadn't spent a day in the Majors. In the fantasy of baseball—not unlike that of Hollywood—you find a guy so talented and so ridden with star power that he just becomes so firmly fixed in the dream of a franchise that he is seen as a player who will one day be written in the team's history the way that Joe DiMaggio and Roberto Clemente and Stan Musial are recalled.

The trouble was Jake Swain could not speak, like Echo in the Greek myths Jake could only utter the last word spoken to him. The catcher to Jake: "throw your curve." "Curve," Jake responded.

The impediment had been with Jake since age 8 around the time he started fourth grade at the Bill Templeton Elementary school in Delmarva, some 50 miles east of Baltimore. Delmarva, for those who don't know it, is a peninsula surrounded by Delaware, Maryland and Virginia That's where the name comes from. DEL-MAR-VA.

Before the disability Jake seemed somewhat normal, if a bit odd, shy and withdrawn, stuck mostly with his head buried in books. Despite that, the some kids in school may have thought of him as retarded At the same school, two grades up was Lyle Hunter, today one of the Norfolk Seagulls' starting pitchers. Lyle and Jake lived on the same shoreline area. The boys played ball together even if Lyle was older because the kids noticed Jake had skills and could throw a baseball more than 60 yards. He was encouraged to be a part of the after school sandlot baseball team, sponsored by Delmarva Motors, the Ford franchise in town And his acceptance had nothing to do with the fact that Jake's dad had baseball cards printed up with all the guys pictured. full head and shoulder on one side and bat in hand or fielding a position on the other. Jake could straight out play.

'Where's he gonna play?"

"Why with that arm, pitcher, where else?" Lyle said.

"But you're the pitcher, Lyle--"

"Relief pitcher then."

Jake's father got rich on fat 10 years ago. He had the date he had realized he was well-to-do circled on a framed Calendar page from 1957 in his office. Success started for Eric Swain when he drove all around Maryland collecting fat from butcher shops and farms.. With his packed van he would go to fast food restaurants and sell the collected fat. In a year's time, he was the major distributor of lard in Maryland and parts of Virginia. His company was called Fry Easy, Inc.. One could imagine how well off a firm can be if it had the likes of MacDonald, Burger King, Denny's and Wendy's as customers. I guess people around Delmarva knew that the Swains were German descent, as many American are. Actually, their name was reinvented after the the war to Swain when Jake's father came here from Nazi Germany, one of the World War II refugees.

Jake once asked his dad, "What did you do during the war?"

"I served under Field Marshall Rommel in North Africa. I was captured at age 17 by the Americans and sent to prison camp in war-torn Germany. After the war, I was set free. And I was a penniless waif wandering in battered Berlin and by the grace of god I fell in with Eleanor Roosevelt's refugee program."

So now with money no object and with Jake's changed circumstance his father, Eric, sought help for his son at the neurological departments of Johns Hopkins and George Washington Hospital and had even inquired after the popular writer and neurologist. Oliver Sacks, but Dr. Sacks was dying of cancer.

LYLE HUNTER

I gotta say I was so happy to see Jake join us in Norfolk. It was in May 1972. He came in with a huge grin on his face. People back home use to say with that smile on his handsome face he'll have to blow off all the Hollywood agents, drooling to sign him up for the pictures. Well, maybe that could of happened when the movies were silent because Jake ...well you know or heard.

Jake and I were pals for a long time. When shit happened, it took me a while to get used to his not saying anything but in no time it became normal like a kid with a twisted lip or a limp. You get used to it and really, you don't see it.

I looked forward to playing ball with him, that million dollar arm, even as a kid. I guess if it wasn't against age restrictions, baseball organizations would have signed him at 10 years old.

Yeah, I pitched too, but Jake was better than me. Hard to admit 'cause I take pride in my pitching but when he walked into camp at Norfolk, I knew I wouldn't be the team ace.

It was me who got him into organized ball. I was playing for the Frederick Falcons in Class A and I told my manager, Bill Brinker, about him. He just nodded and all I could do was wait. Maybe Brinker told the guy in charge of scouting, Next thing I heard they signed Jake but he didn't have to go far. They sent him to the Delmarva Ponies, short season A Ball. You have to be a local to know where the word Ponies comes from. The legend has it that in the 17th Century a Spanish galleon sunk in the peninsula. The sailing vessel had horses aboard who swam to the island and over the centuries of inbreeding shrunk down to pony size.

What can I tell you about Jake? He was Mr. Perfect, except for the speech thing, his Achilles heel. He was popular here in Norfolk. The speech thing was hardly anything when you think there were major league stars who played with all sorts of handicaps like the guy with a deformed right hand who pitched a no-hitter and there were guys with clubbed feet and if you go back in history there was Mordecai Brown with 40% of his fingers missing. And there were guys who were outright whacky like Rube Waddell who chased fire engines and left the mound in the middle of a game to go fishing. And there was Eddie Gaedel, 3 feet 7 inches.

Yeah, he was a publicity stunt but he still set the major league record for On Base Percentage and Consecutive Walks. Nobody could pitch to him.

Some might want to ask about how Jake got along with girls. It might be true that women like the strong silent type. I don't know. We've got hot cheerleaders here, wiggle their fannies at intermission while announcers sell shit. I know some of them. One is called Dixie and she took one big shine to Jake. let me tell you. Jake was my roommate. Of course, he couldn't warn me to stay away. I walked in our place and caught Dixie on top of Jake pumping away and loving it, her head back. panting, looked like she was about to pass out from delight. I tip-toed out.

Dixie must have known I had come in because she stopped me a day or two later.

"Lyle, you gotta minute."

"Yeah sure," I said.

"Well this is embarrassing but does Jake have a lotta girls. You caught us."

"Dixie, don't worry. I ain't gonna tell anyone."

"Who are the others, Lyle?"

"I don't know. I really don't."

I wasn't lying. Jake was the mystery of mysteries. If he was fucking some of the other cheer leaders or girls in town I didn't know. It's easy to get your rocks off in Norfork. It's a sailor's town, a US Navy port. All you gotta do is walk into a bar and one of the hookers come right up to you and caress your crotch. Two minutes later she'll spread her legs or blow you for 50 or 75 bucks, or more, in case you want something kinky, or want her for the whole night. That's what the guys tell me.

"It seems like he'd known some others. Surely you must know. He's been around women.," Dixie persisted.

"Yeah, of course. He's got two sisters, a Mom and a Grandma."

"Lyle, please—"

I shrugged and walked away.

All the time I've known Jake, he'll surprise you. In grade school the teachers couldn't believe how much he knew or how fast he caught on. He was a math whizz in school and he could read and comprehend. I don't know how they judged his understanding with his disability. But there are ways. For one, Jake could write a blue streak and he always could read and tell—I mean write-- what the story was about. A lot of kids fumbled the ball on that.

DIXIE JANE LOGAN

Jake was best guy I'd ever been with. There been some others, three or four Seagulls, over the past two years. But, wow, Jake was night and day. The others throw you on the bed or jump you against the wall, pump away for about a minute and that was So long Charlie, all spent.

Jake was a long distance runner, get off slowly, with the best kissing, glide into forepay, touch the right places till I'm tingly and all wet down there and then, bursting as I am, Jake put his thing in me and I trembled with delight. I was afraid I'd scare him off. But no, Jake just continued with that rhythm of his and I wondered if my heart would burst from the thrill. He was on top of me and I was on top of him and I came so many times I can't count.

"Don't stop," I said breathlessly

"Stop," he said.

*I can't stop. Please, Jake. Don't stop. Don't."

"Don't," he said. And I remembered his disability. And we went on, till finally I had to ease him off. I don't think girls have dreams that good even when they're playing with themselves.

Pity was we couldn't talk to each other and I could never hear the magic word from him that I longed for, I love you.

I haven't given up; I smile when I see him, caress his cheek, show him just the tip of my tongue. And he smiles back, and I die.

MISS LUCY CARTER, M.ED

I had Jake in my English class at Delmarva High School. We teachers had all been told about his problem from reports from Templeton grade school so we weren't thrown by his one word utterances. One of my extra duties was reviewing student reports from the other teachers. I think I got that handed me because I had a graduate degree in ED from the University of Maryland. So, as I was strapped with more than a bachelor's degree and a teaching license they found extra assignments for me.

How do I tell you about Jake Swain? In my class we did language arts – grammar, vocabulary, lit and comp, the typical curriculum in 8th Grade. But being as I had the blown up degree I threw myths, dramas, novels, short stories and poetry at the kids.

Jake always surprised me. I had been talking about conjugating verbs –infinitive , past and past participle.

And the following day I gave the class a test, listing infinite verbs and asking them to tell the past and past participle. It wasn't an easy test and, as expected, most of the class messed up some. Jake? Jake was perfect He wrote:

> **do** did done
> **Cut** cut cut
> **Drink** drank drunk
> **Fall** fell fallen
> **Forsake** forsook forsaken

And when you come to reading comprehension, Jake was unbelievable. The class was assigned to read a book and tell about it. Jake, of course, was allowed write about it. Had no trouble there. Excellent writer— good grammar and spelling, as you can imagine, way above grade level. Because of his not being able to speak. I can't say I got to know the real Jake, even though I was tempted to write about him. But to write about Jake is to write about someone larger than life, and all editors will tell you, stories are about people one can recognize.

Anyway, it was time to collect the class assignments. I was thrown because Jake had chosen Dostoyevsky's *Crime and Punishment.* Surprised me because that novel might be discussed in college at advanced literature classes.

And I didn't even know where Jake got hold of it. I knew he had two sisters in college. So maybe there.

Want to be bowled over. Here is what Jake turned in, a report that would put most college students to shame written in a style very few could imagine—in second person..

Crime and Punishment

You're Rodion Rashkolnikov and you think you believe in God. You're a destitute and talented former student wandering on streets of St. Petersburg practicing vows in silence and anger.

You're Rodion Rashkolinkov with shame at the inability to care for your family; so, you commit a vile act because you feel it is justified because of the good it would incur in "killing a louse".

So, you bash the old pawnbroker's head in because you seem to believe only the sin of murder and unconditional submission to God will save your soul.

You're Rodion Rashkolnikov and you killed knowing that in our Christian society there are no perfect crimes because the killer's guilt prevents it. The murderer is compelled to leave clues and so, in this way, a terrible sin confessed.

You're Rodion Rashkolnikov and you are condemned.

Jakob Swain

Okay, my larger than life Jake takes math and here is his math teacher's report:

Jakob Swain Grade A+

Algebra I excellent.
Geometry excellent

Student excellent in real numbers, rational and irrational numbers and integers, variables, exponents and powers.

Student understands lines, slopes, and the Pythagorean Theorem.

Able to simplify and rewrite equations to solve problems.

And his Social Studies report found Jacob Swain attentive in studies that encompass history. culture. people. Fond of World War II and quickly learned the officials of the US Army from Eisenhower to MacArthur to Bradley and the Third Reich, from Hitler to Himmler to Rudolf Hess.

Jacob Swain is reported to be a normal art student in drawing, photography and graphic design.

So much for the greater than life Jake Swain. He was a student way ahead of the others to say the very least.

ERIC SWAIN

How can a parent be happy with a child's disability? It came on so suddenly, out of the blue. One day normal, no exceptional, and the next, struck dumb. My boy unable to speak. I'm a successful businessman; I've got money in the back, lots of it. I had to find answers. So, I took Jake on a journey into neurology, sought out the best doctors looked them up in *The Best Doctors* book and made appointments. First with team a George Washington University Hospital. They studied him, found nothing physical to have caused his disability. Next with Lionel Long, MD, PhD at Johns Hopkins. Put Jake through two weeks of tests.

"I can't find anything wrong. Did every test in the book and then some. There is nothing abnormal except...well you know." Dr Long said, throwing open his arms, perhaps in surrender.

"Did you review Dr. Sacks studies. See if there was anything in those cases that could help Jake?" I asked.

Dr. Long took a deep breath before telling me, "Dr. Sacks delved into the nuances of neurology in a captivating way to doctors and his readers, reporting case histories of patients with weird, bizarre neurological conditions. I've read all his books, trust me."

"And?"

"And none of his cases are like Jake. Jake doesn't fit."

"I read he had some success with L-Dopa—"

"Yes, with psychiatric patients in a trance-like state, the lingering effect of an encephalitis lethargica epidemic that raged after World War I."

"So, did you try L-Dopa on my son?"

"No, Jake has no such symptoms."

"Surely it was worth a try."

"Mr. Swain, L-Dopa has side effects—abnormal heart rate, aggressive behavior, excessive nausea, vomiting, mood change, depression. Jake didn't fit and he wasn't going to get L-Dopa from me."

"What can we do?"

"His problem, in my opinion, is psychiatric. He may have perceived some horrible trauma which caused his condition."

"You have a doctor in mind--?"

"It may take more than one."

"Why?"

"Jake has to find a doctor he is comfortable with."

"Don't they all treat the same?"

"You go to buy a suit of clothes. Mr. Swain. You look through the racks. And Voila! You love the blue pin-stripe."

As I was leaving, he said, "Stay cool. Jake's doing fine. He's made adjustments. The world around him has adjusted as well."

J.R. JOHNSTONE MD, PHD.

Jake Swain was referred to me by an older colleague, Dr. William Leyer, who was retiring after 40 years of practice. He was Jake Swain's third psychiatrist. Jake had been a new patient of his for only a month. Dr. Leyer reported that Jake Swain was a calm young man of high intelligence who was willing to write answers to questions.

"I have found nothing aberrant, except the apparent loss of speech. All our sessions had been pleasant, though I did note that he seemed hesitant to write about his family."

So maybe exploring the family will bring us closer to what caused the disability.

I was late for my appointment keeping Jake and my earlier appointment waiting as I was unable to reach them by phone. The patient before Jake had fallen into a depression over work. He was glaring at Jake when I came in and only learned later what happened.

"I went up to the guy, stuck out my hand and said, 'David Essich."

"Essich," he said.

"Yeah, what's your name?"

"Name?"

"What are you mocking me?"

"Me"

"Ah, Fuck!!"

"Fuck" he answered.

He was a big athletic guy. He stood up. That's when you came in." Essich said.

"David, he's a minor league baseball player for the Norfolk Seagulls in the International League. He can't speak except only the last word said to him."

"Oh, shit. I thought he was making fun of me."

"He's really a nice guy."

Then David told me he had brought along a document that he had gotten from Soviet archives during World War II. This was the file that had driven him crazy while working for the Simon Wiesenthal Nazi hunting section. He hoped I would read it and maybe find something in it .

"It was originally in German but I translated it," Essich said."twenty-five pages."

"That will be helpful. I'll read it tonight."

"Maybe I should wait till you finished it, but the fucking thing has been haunting me."

"I know."

"I spent a month in Moscow, tracking down an escaped Nazi, finally some KGB officer told me of an investigation that had been carrried out just after the war by a Soviet Major, Irina Pedrova, who is also KGB."

"I see, David. It's important, a lot of digging."

"Yeah, since we still haven.t caught the guy."

"I'll read it tonight. Catch you tomorrow."

"Let me ask you. Should I apologize to the guy in the waiting room?"

"No need. I'm sure he's forgiven you. That kind of thing has been a part of his life."

When Jake entered the office, I asked him if he was troubled by Essich.

He shook his head, no.

"Everyday stuff for you?"

Jake nodded. I was pleased he didn't repeat the last word I said.

We had made that much progress in our sessions. It was a good sign. When he wanted to speak he used a pad to write on.

Jake wrote: *I know about him--Essich..*

"Really? How?"

He wrote: *I saw him on the Hitsory Channel about Simon Wiesenthal's endeaavors and their connection to Israel's Mossad.*

"Yes, you've always been interested in the War."

Jake nodded.

"Why is that?"

Jake didn't respond.

"Well, maybe one day you'll write about it."

I wondered if that facination was the key to his disability. I knew I'd have to be patient, bide my time till it became clearer. Still, I ventured forward.

During the war, I was in Naval Intelligence, spying on the Stasi. Have you heard of them?"

Jake nodded then wrote: *East German secret service.*

"Not many people your age are so well-informed. How'd you learn about the Stasi? History Channel or read about them?

Jake wrote: *Both . I was surprised to learn that many of the Stasi were former Gestapo and SS.*

"Wow. I'm impresed. Why was that do you think?"

Jake took up the pad again. *Trying to save their asses.*

Can't beat 'em, join 'em.

"But they had been fervent Nazis," I probed, see where it would take us.

Jake said nothing for the next 30 seconds or so. Then he started writing: *What I can't understand why the millions of Germans went along with Hitler.*

"Some historians are puzzled by that too. After World War I things were really bad. Shortages, recession, people out of work, going hungry, no hopes and along came Hitler."

Jake wrote: *Were they Nazis underneath?*

"Desperate," I told him.

Our session was over.

DET. GIL TOTTEN

The call that a business man in Central Islip, Long Island, New York was found in his home clubbed on the head then strangled had come into the precinct on the same day the Long Island Ducks in the Atlantic League were playing an exhibition game with the Norfolk Seagulls Triple A team in the Baltimore organization. The Ducks had won the prestigious Ferry Cup three seasons in a row, a trophy named after the Ferry Transportation company that carried people back and forth from Bridgeport, Connecticut to Central Islip. I was at the game when police station filled me in.

I didn't mind the interruption because the Norfolk pitcher, Jake Swain, was mowing the Ducks down, five innings of no-hit ball, nine strikeouts. Embarrassing. Wally Backman, the Ducks manger and former New York Mets second baseman, ordered the whole team to bunt. But the Seahawks were up for it, as it might have been a trick other teams had tried on Jake Swain. They gobbled up the bunts and lights out.

I went to the dead man's home on Millrun Road along with the crime scene guys. There were two officers already at the house.

"Who found the body?" I asked the policeman nearest the opened door.

"He's inside," the cop told him, "local handyman. He'd come to hang the storm windows, does it every year around this time."

"Who let him in?"

"Nobody," the garage was open, storm windows were stored there. He just set up the ladder and started hanging till he got to the living room and saw the victim on the floor and the blood."

"You got an ID on the corpse?"

"Yeah, local business man, Alvin Curtis, heating and cooling business. Company seemed to have been connected to General Electric.

"Yeah, I know the place. There's a showroom on Indian Creek Drive. The company sells GE products -- stoves, furnaces. vents, air conditioner all that."

I went into the Vic's house. There wasn't that much blood -- spread under Curtis's head I guessed that Curtis was alive before he was strangled

The crime scene boys were around the body.

"Whaddya find in his pockets?" I asked.

"Address book, $83 cash, wallet, driver's license. On the desk there's a business accounts ledger."

I went over, opened the book, saw a month's profits and losses. As I went through the ledger I was astounded to find Curtis' company, CAN Heating and Cooling, had done close to ¾ of a million dollars in business. I didn't believe it.. I suspected the books were cooked, but why would a company show so much earnings when it would lead to huge income taxes. The bank statements were on another page. $318,000 in Chase and $176.000 In Long Island Trust. How the fuck?!! Their store, okay showroom, wasn't that big. As I turned the pages, it was clear the victim had two employees—Joe Cook and Fred Russo, locals I didn't know. At some point I'd have to talk to them.

"When can I get a look at the address book? "I asked one of the forensic guys.

"When we're finished with it at the lab."

I turned to the coroner, Johnny Doscher."

"Strangled or killed by the blow?"

"Johnny Doscher said. "Somebody whacked him on the side of the head. There's a skull injury. Something blunt with an edge. Figure he was knocked out then choked"

I looked around, my eyes stopping at a wooden box on the mantelpiece.

"Yeah," Doscher said, "we're going to take that to the lab. Seem to be war souvenirs, a bunch of Nazi medals and ribbons, swastika arm band. We'll look for prints, traces of blood, you know."

"Think the corpse was a veteran, then?"

"Could be, but there must have been 20-30 Alvin Curtises in the military during the War. You going to check on that?" Doscher asked.

"Yeah, but don't know where to start.."

"You'll figure it out." Doscher said..

"I'm going to look around. Okay?"

Doscher saw I had followed crime scene protocol – my shoes wrapped and wearing surgical gloves.

"Okay, Totten." He handed me a tweezers. plastic evidence bags. "See that you don't fuck things up."

"Ain't the room contaminated already?" I asked.

"We've taken everybody's shoes and prints." Doscher told me.

I opened the business ledger again. Copied the employees names, their social security numbers, addresses and phone numbers.

Then I picked up the souvenier box. Just like Doscher said. A lot of Nazi stuff---medals, Iron crosses all with swastika embossed, arm band, even a captured German Luger. In the barrel I spotted a piece of paper, tweezered it out. Two phone numbers were written. Beside the numbers were a series of letters and symbols that didn't make sense like strong passwords. Whlt3hOr531iev3M and L#G$ _TM4+! I copied it all down.

"I'll be at the station," I told the crime crew.

I called the number for Joe Cook. A male voice answered.

"I'm a detective, Gil Totten. You work for Alvin Curtis?"

"Yeah, sounds like there's trouble." the voice on the phone said.

"Big trouble. Your boss has been murdered."

"Whaaaat? Wait!" I heard him call out: "Frank, come here! Mr. Curtis has been killed."

"Mr. Cook, you're with Frank Russo right now?"

"Yeah, we were having a barbecue."

"I need to talk to you both. I'm at the police station. I need you both to come down. Ask for Gil Totten".

When Cook and Russo arrived, they were brought to me. Both looked kind of shaken.

"I'm homicide as you can imagine. What is it you do for the company?"

"We help with sales when we're not out on call," Russo answered.

"On call?"

"We're both graduates of the training school some companies formed to help with their products. Mr. Curtis has been selling these their stuff for years. We answer service calls answer service calls," Cook explained.

"His own personal repair men then?"

"Yeah," Russo answered nervously, "we install and fix furnaces, hot water heaters, thermostats, heat pumps, blower motors. help with flashing errors lights and heaters blowing cold air."

"Only GE?"

"No, we install many brands--American Standard, Carrier, Thane, Lennox. It depends what the customer wants to spend. We'll sell them GE if they don't specify.

I held up my hand. "Okay, Okay. I get it. GE is number one."

Cook said, "we sometimes cover Riverhead up East and the branch at the Water Mill mall in the Hamptons. Mr. Curtis has partners there."

Same deal with these companies in Riverhead and Water Mill?"

"They may vary a little."

"Did the partners get along?"

"I guess. They'd argue every now and then, like all partners." Russo said.

"What they argue about? Do you know?"

"No. Just business spats."

"What's the partners names?"

"Lenard Kramer. He's on Hill Street in Riverhead. and Aaron Jacobson, in Water Mill."

"Mr. Jacobson has a couple of guys like us." Cook said. We 're the agents for GE and the others for the whole Long Island."

"Did Curtis run the show?"

"No, he was more of an accountant," Russo said. " Mr. Jacobson was the main boss."

I thanked the two guys for their cooperation.

"One last thing: Did Curtis have any enemies you know of?"

"No, He's been private this past year since his wife, Rosemary, died. Kept to himself. Just stuck to business."

I still had a shit load of work to do. I caught up with the storm window guy. He seemed innocent enough, mentally slow but seemingly harmless.

I checked with military war records. There were 23 Alvin Curtis's spread out over the country and 9 killed in action. I sent the victim's finger prints but no matches turned up, so the victim hadn't served.

My interview with Leonard Kramer gave me nothing that helped. Only odd thing was that he wasn't American, had an accent, maybe German, Dutch, Northern European..

I didn't bother about that at first, but then the foreign accent was bugging me.

So, I went back to see him and bingo!! Leonard Kramer was dead. Garroted. Two dead partners. More work to do. The police in Suffolk County weren't the most cooperative, I'd heard they caught some shit for rough handling of suspects. Maybe the flak turned them off.

DR. J.R. JOHNSTONE

I read David's document from the Russians last night. I was a grueling document, a picture of two unrepentant Nazis.

March 21, 1945.

This is a 25 page transcript of a Soviet investagation of the men who buit the ovens at various death camps. The interrogation is being carried out by Major Irina Pedrova, Soviet Secret Service.

Much has been talked about the Holocaust and "The Final Solution." We explore the minds and reasoning of men who designed and built the cremation ovens at Auschwitz-Birkenau, Buchenwald, Dachau and other extermination camps where more than six million people were murdered.

Our Soviet Army had records captured from concentration camps which pointed us to this investigation of Heizrohr and Sohne, furnace makers.

From captured papers:

SPEIEGELGRUND CLINIC - VIENNA - DAY (1940)

This Vienna clinic, like others euthanasia facilities in Germany -- at Hartheim, Hadamar Sonnenstein -- has been established to carry out experiments on thousands of children deemed by the Nazi government to be physically, mentally or otherwise unfit for Hitler's vision of the Third Reich. It was all perfectly legal and sanctified by the Church five years ago under the <u>Erbgesundheitgesetz,</u> a law to safeguard the health of the German people.

Ernst Heizrohr the owner, and Hans Schweinbauer, chief Engineer of the company, had visited the clinic to determine what sort of oven would be required to handle the cremation of the unwanted.

Both are present in the interrogation room at Soviet Station, interview room B. Brandenburg, Germany.

Major Pedrova

I want both of you in the room.

Let's see Hans Schweinbauer, Chief Engineer for the company, joined the National Socialists practically before you were asked to. Eager to sign up with the Führer, were you?

Schweinbauer

All good Germans joined the National Socialists. Why are you questioning us? The American Third Army met with us and found us blameless. In fact, they hired us to fix the heating at their headquarters.

Pedrova

We are investigating war crimes. War crimes are defined broadly. Of course, the Nazi SS has been declared a criminal organization guilty of exterminating and persecuting Jews and killing prisoners-of-war and slave laborers.

Schweinbauer

We were not SS.

Pedrova

But you should also know that a war criminal is defined as anyone who was a principal, accessory to, or consented in the commission of war crimes, or anyone who was a member of an organization or group connected with the commission or sanction of such crimes.

Schweinbauer

Shouldn't we have legal representation?

Pedrova

That will come when and if we charge you with war crimes. At this moment I am confirming the affidavits you gave to the American Third Army and the files captured at Dachau and elsewhere. Putting punctuation on what we've found.

Schweinbauer

Soviet punctuation?

Pedrova

We'll begin now, Ernst Heizrohr. as we understand it, your company was started by your grandfather. Your father and uncle ran it till World War I, when both were killed in France. Your Grandfather took over again and stayed in that role until you were named Director.

Then you hired Hans Schweinbauer in 1935. None of you served in the Nazi military.

Pedrova

The captured records show things went well for Heizrohr and Sohne and, then, from 1938 on business got even better! You got some new orders, new consultation fees from the General Foundation for Institutional Care. The headquarters of this foundation was in an exclusive section of Berlin. You were invited to report to Tiergartenstrasse 4 for a meeting. Did you know then what Tiergartenstrasse 4 was?

Heizrohr

We were summoned to Berlin by the Führer Chancellery. Couldn't very well refuse. After all, the Chancellery...

Pedrova

So, you knew what T-4 was?

Heizrohr

It was hush-hush. SS, Gestapo, high courts. Occasionally one heard T4 referred to in some private government doings. But what went on there was not really known. Not by us, anyway.

Pedrova

Five years ago, as you know, the Nazis set out to establish a community of the true German people. And I don't have to tell you that meant unburdening of social outsiders including all the so-called problem cases and the chronically ill. You got to T4 there and were told they were planning to conduct a cleaning out of unwanted populations, a euthanasia program.

Heizrohr

I'm prepared to answer. I was introduced to some doctors who would making decisions about the patients. These were top people. There were also church people in the room, a Bishop smiling benignly.

Pedrova

They signed on, the church people? They were part of the elimination of the unwanted?

Heizrohr

They were present. I didn't ask their part. All I know is that the priests nodded when the doctors told me that every patient in the program would be studied diligently.

Pedrova

Studied diligently? Did they tell you how?

Heizrohr

They explained that a series of tests would be carried out and that at least two doctors would sign off on who was absolutely incurable.

PEDROVA

What was your first reaction, then?

Heizrohr

I didn't know what to say. Then I told the SS officer that, yes, we didn't understand why we were chosen to build the <u>Krema</u>.

Pedrova

How did the SS react?

Schweinbauer

If I may, they were not really troubled. We were told that their asking us to take this assignment showed proof that they could count on us, the people in our company. We'd be given a top rating, though we wouldn't have anything to do with the program. We would merely build the <u>Krema.</u>

Pedrova

Top rating meant you'd be considered indispensable and, therefore, protected?

Schweinbauer

Yes.

Pedrova

You'd be building crematoria for people who were going to be killed? You weren't bothered?

Schweinbauer

Well, you see, We didn't allow ourselves to dwell on it because they explained the program would be carried out by these important doctors who were in charge of the nation's health.

Pedrova

Sounds like you were given a choice, were you, Heizrohr.?

Heizrohr

I had no choice! Several times they mentioned that the health of Germany was at issue. My company had the technical expertise. Didn't I care about the nation's health?

Pedrova

How did they know you had the expertise? Advertised it, did you? Or did you actually volunteer? Bring Schweinbauer with you to sell yourself?

Heizrohr

They contacted me, asked me to bring Hans along.

Pedrova

Let's turn to Herr Schweinbauer. You were at a meeting at Tiergartenstrasse 4 with the euthanasia group. You were a member of the National Socialist,

Schweinbauer

One had to be. Yes, I wanted to join the party

Pedrova

May I ask, why?

I grew up in a family that was very much aware of race. My parents felt the country was going to the dogs – degeneration, moral decay. I was a young man, suggestible, I guess. The National Socialists seemed right, a way to correct the ills. And there was the threat of—-

Pedrova

The threat of what? Communism?

Schweinbauer

Yes. We were afraid of it over running our society. I'm sorry to say this to you. I know you must be faithful to the land of your fathers. And I was too.

Pedrova

So, the Third Reich didn't turn you off. The Nazis' ideas were okay with you. Was there a social consensus in support of Hitler and the Nazis?

Schweinbauer

I don't know about any social consensus.

Pedrova

I mean the Germans didn't need orders to follow. They did it willingly.

Schweinbauer

Little people, big people, intellectuals participated in the war effort...as far as I could tell. Everybody served.

Pedrova

So there you and Heizrohr are in Berlin, at T-4, with the euthanasia committee, two men with children of your own, and what is being proposed is the incineration of children with maladies all of whom had been labeled <u>Rückkehr nicht erwünscht</u> -- return not desired -- and neither of you stop to think, what if it was my child?

Heizrohr

We were told that the merciful euthanasia program was justified, and that it would be carried out on careful medical grounds with the permission of the parents.

Pedrova

Nonsense! You knew what it was all about. They had to tell you about the euthanasia institutes, as they called them, gassings would take place. You built crematoria in 3 or 4 special sections. Did you ever ask if any of the patients they examined were returned to their families?

Heizrohr

Ours was an engineering assignment. We were not medical experts, or sociologists. It would be an inappropriate question to ask.

Pedrova

You remained disengaged? You were without any moral discernment? So, both of you knew what was being planned at T-4. You knew they weren't conducting some merciful program of assisted suicide for a handful of malformed, terminal misfortunates.

Heizrohr

We didn't look into it that deeply. Only the Krema.

Pedrova

But you saw the set up at least 3 of their units you built and serviced the Krema. You knew what was going on. These weren't only people on their last legs lying in bed with empty eyes in their hospital gowns, pleading to be put down.

The fact is there were not only very sick people in the euthanasia program. Later on, you also saw there were some Jews and Gypsies and later homosexuals and political people with unbecoming attitudes, or people who had contravened the Nazi race laws. Didn't you ever ask who are all these patients being put down.

Heizrohr

*We knew inappropriate curiosity could get you in trouble.
We plunged into the technical aspects of the furnaces.*

Pedrova

*But you saw the patients. Did they make them wear
differently colored inverted triangles on their gowns
with pink for homosexual and purple for Jehovah's
Witness, and blue for emigrant? How many Jewish
stars did you see? Or didn't they use these symbols in
the training camps?*

Schweinbauer

What training camps?

Pedrova

*Surely, at some point, it must have occurred to both of
you that these euthanasia sections were training units
for the death camps to come... And that you were all
honing your skills for Dachau, and Auschwitz-Birkenau
and Buchenwald and the rest.*

Schweinbauer

It was all very legal. We were told that judges drafted several confidential legal memoranda that sanctioned the program. They showed us the documents.

Pedrova

No, actually the SS went forum shopping for those opinions. There were, in fact, a few German judges who opposed the Euthanasia Program on legal grounds.

Heizrohr

We only knew what we were told by the officials and the doctors. The said the patients were no good to themselves and a drain on the country's economy. At best they would only live a short while. Their plan was to deliver them from misery.

Pedrova

No, their plan was the legalized extermination of the undesirables, what the Nazis called the inferiors, the dregs and the rabble. And all of you were part of it. You knew what they were doing was vile and unconscionable. It must have occurred to you that you must remove yourself from this mass murder.

Heizrohr

We knew none of this! We were not lawyers or doctors. We knew nothing!

Pedrova

But then it all became very clear. Over the next couple of years, you were consulted as Krema engineers in the building of five extermination camps.

Heizrohr

We were told the bodies were being burned there were for sanitary reasons. The dead were prisoners of the state who had succumbed to disease.

Pedrova

But you knew better, didn't you? Because the doctors in the euthanasia program had told you all the tests were fake, all the evaluations were once-over lightly. Or did they just wink? And you saw when you visited these euthanasia setups that no patients were returned to their families, except in cardboard boxes that passed for urns.

Heizrohr

We were engineers. We were not engaged with the parents. We were not involved in patient treatment.

Pedrova

There was no treatment. The treatment was gassing. Or the inoculation of fatal chemicals. That was the plan. The euthanasia units were laboratories to train people for mass murder. And you knew that when you moved on to the extermination camps with your <u>Krema</u>.

Heizrohr

Not true! We knew nothing of the sort.

Pedrova

And didn't you also look at film of people being gassed.

Heizrohr

There was no filming of people dying. I understood that doctors had some slits, these little windows, to tell when it was over.

Pedrova

You only saw how the corpses were shoveled into the Krema, right? But were these viewings only for technical study or were they part of the desensitization aspect. After all, you had work to carry out in Auschwitz.

Heizrohr

We were not schooled to accept death. We were just engineers.

Pedrova

Well, if you were not schooled, trained, conditioned for work in the death camps then one can only conclude you were volunteers because your natures were particularly suited to mass murder.

Schweinbauer

I was the chief engineer from about 1937 to the present. I built the furnaces at Auschwitz. Before that I designed smaller furnaces for the euthanasia program. Ernst was the initial contacts.

Pedrova

You mean Heizrohr brought in the business?

Schweinbauer

They sought his advice.

Pedrova

They?

Schweinbauer

The Waffen SS. I didn't deal with the SS at all. I consulted with Heizrohr in the design of the furnaces.

Pedrova

How often did you visit Auschwitz and why did you visit?

Schweinbauer

A few times, maybe a half dozen in the beginning in 1940 to 43. The first was to receive orders about where the Krema were to be situated. Then to look at the site. After that I went to check on a fault in the chimney. Then, there were inspection trips. The last time was in

*the fall of 1944 because the camp commander wanted
to move the Krema...the front was getting closer.*

Pedrova

So, you must have watched the Krema operate--

Schweinbauer

*On one morning I saw them prepare the corpses – men,
women and children of different ages – for incineration.*

Pedrova

How did that affect you?

Schweinbauer

*Affect me? I had an engineering problem. I had to see the
pathways of the corpses to determine what to advise.*

Pedrova

You saw the Jews gassed?

Schweinbauer

I knew there were gas chambers.

Pedrova

And what did you think?

Schweinbauer

Sickness. Jews struggling for life. Why delay their agony, you see? I didn't think of it as murder. I thought of it as gassing people for health reasons, sanitary reasons. Anyway, I was there to look at the functioning of the furnaces. I didn't make decisions on who was to be gassed, and for what reasons.

Pedrova

But privately you must have had some qualms...and then when they asked you to build and attend to the Krema at other camps -- Buchenwald, Dachau, Treblinka – how did you react?

Schweinbauer

Well, you see, whatever I felt, I knew that I was a contract employee with Heizrohr und Söhne, instructed to design and build three muffle furnaces, and I was aware that the work was important to the Reich... And there was the possibility of being killed myself if I refused.

Pedrova

Are you saying you went on building them out of fear for your life?

Schweinbauer

My life wasn't actually threatened. I was told by Heizrohr that it was an order from the SS Command, and that there was an urgency to complete the order.

Pedrova

Did the ovens breakdown?

Schweinbauer

Well, of course. You see they had the gas chambers right next door. And they got these thick, brawny peasants from Poland and the Ukraine and trained them to push hundreds of Jews at a time into the room with a capacity for a third of that.

Pedrova

Then they squeezed them into the ovens too?

Schweinbauer

Sure, even you can imagine what a problem it created. The linings of the furnace couldn't take the stain. They pushed the Jews in maybe a dozen times a day. What did you expect? The Krema had to give out. I didn't design them for that kind of a load.

Pedrova

At any time did you know that innocent people were being gassed and burned?

Schweinbauer

I came to know. In the beginning I just accepted what I was told about these sick people. But then you had to be an absolute <u>dummkopf</u> not to know they were killing the Jews the unwanted, and political enemies.

Pedrova

But you knew before. Stories about the concentration camps were widely reported in the press. Hitler never tried to hide it.

Schweinbauer

Yes, but that was for social outsiders.

Pedrova

A long list of social outsiders wasn't it? Let's see. Jews. Gypsies, criminals, prostitutes, foreign workers, homosexuals, the chronically ill. How did that make you feel?

Schweinbauer

What could I do? I was under pressure. I was under orders. The furnaces were failing from the overloading. I couldn't let myself think of anything else. I threw myself into the engineering.

Pedrova

You were worried about your reputation. What was it, each day another 12000 human beings were railed in to Auschwitz?

Schweinbauer

Ah, so finally you see the problem. Who can maintain a reputation with that load. You want to know what I thought of? I thought of mean temperature differential, heat transfer, radiation emission and heat loss through the furnace walls. That's all I could think about.

Pedrova

But on a human level, you must have thought these poor people had been herded into box cars, unloaded at extermination camps, separated from their families, abused. Surely, you saw they were terrified, wondering what next, what was in store for them.

Schweinbauer

I couldn't save the Jews. Look, I accepted that I was helping Germany win the war. I was a German furnace engineer. No different from a rocket scientist whose designs are used to kill our country's enemies.

Both were deemed war criminal and sentenced to trial. In Court – Both were sentenced for 5 years, Heizrohr served his time. Schweinbauer seemed to have slipped in with several SS prisoners who were interrogated by the Americans in West Berlin and sent to the US. At the time the Soviets and Americans did exchange prisoners when asked.

I couldn't wait for David to get to our session so we could talk about it. When he was seated he said, "When I got to interview Pedrova she was a Colonel, in her sixties, but looked 10 years younger.. Quite attractive. She told me Heizrohr was no longer alive and hadn't even served his complete sentence. He was released early – because the Soviet prison in Brandenburg was overcrowded. Heizrohr had been killed by an enraged person, unknown, thrown off a bridge. The East German authorities never sought the perpetuator.

Good riddance, I said. And Schweinbauer?

"He fell in with two SS men and was switched to a prison in the American section. Pedrova told me releasing prisoners was common at that time. If the Russians wanted to question a prisoner in the American section the US turned him over and vice versa."

So, they are lost? I asked.

Colonel thought they might have been taken to this country.

Gone forever?

"Not so," David said. "The Mossad has been hunting them."

And?

"And they say not to worry."

So, you should be happy. Why are you still so upset?

"I don't know what the SS men were accused of, but I want to bring Schweinbauer to stand trial in Israel. I don't want the Mossad to just kill him.

I see, I said. But if he is killed by the Mossad it's a kind of justice.

"He's been living here for 30 odd years at peace, untouched, not like the Jews he burnt."

I was trying to help David but he was determined to get his kind of revenge. I asked how far he had gotten.

"I and others at the Center have been tracking the Mossad."

They aren't easy to track.

"We've got help in Israel."

You are putting yourself in danger, David.

"I want that fucking Schweinbauer."

What I don't understand is how they were only sentenced to 5 years, I said.

"Yes, I asked that of Colonel Pedrova and she told me the Russian soldiers had been killing Germans indiscriminately. They'd kill anyone who looked at them cross-eyed and even those who didn't. I think it may have troubled the Russian and they went lenient on Heizrohr and Schweinbauer.

Our session came to a close. Jake Swain was next.

He came in and wrote: *Your patient just apologized.*

I told Jake David felt bad because he didn't know about your condition.

Jake nodded. Then wrote: *You were talking about Nazis?*

Have you been listening again?

He nodded, pointed to his ear.

I told myself to change the time of Jake's appointment so, he doesn't eaves drop anymore..

Jake, this is just instinct --and I'm not supposed to believe in instinct -- but I feel you are getting closer to recovering your speech.

His eyes widened as if asking why I thought that.

You've been writing more and making communicative gestures, I told him. Almost speaking but without the words. I'd like to try something. I'm going to say two words. Please try to repeat them, okay?

He nodded.

God bless, I said.

"God…bless."

Great , Jake, you're doing it.

"Doing… it." He repeated.

You're amazing

"You're amazing," he said. He smiled.

How wonderful.

"Who is Schweinbauer?

What? I was knocked on my ass. Jake Swain found his voice.

GIL TOTTEN

It was clear the murderer of Curtis and Kramer wasn't done yet. There was the guy in the Hamptons. I drove out to Water Mill, found the GE operation in the mall.

A woman approached when I walked in.

"May I help you with something, sir?"

"I'm a detective from Central Islip and I need to see Aaron Jacobson. It's urgent."

"Is it about the partners who were murdered?"

"Yep."

Jacobson was at his desk. He was a man in his seventies with a gray crewcut and deep blue eyes, clean shaven..

I introduced myself and then told him. "You are in danger, sir. Your partners have been murdered. It seems to be revenge killings, something to do with your company, the partnership."

"We've been in business nearly 30 years. Why seek revenge now?"

I told him I had no answer to that. "Maybe someone from the past—"

"The past?"

He looked like he was thinking back.

I told him that they had been in business together, but surely you had to have known each before the business.

Jacobson nodded. "I've hired security. They are here now unobserved. My house is wired for anything you can imagine, detective. I've got two German Shepherds. He opened his desk drawer and pulled out a Glock. I keep this weapon with me at all times."

"I'm on the Curtis case. The killer left no prints, no evidence, except a club he seems to have hit Curtis with but no mis-steps. He entered, hit Curtis over the head then strangled him and left. Professional. And Kramer was garroted.

"So, what should I do, go in a bubble?"

Consider your enemies of the past, Mr. Jacobson. You might find the killer there, I told him.

"They are probably all dead" He had a far-away look in his eyes.

If you think of anyone— I said, and handed him my card.

You've got an accent of some sort, I said. Where are you from?

"The Hamptons. I live in Southampton."

It's not a Long Island accent.

"Not uncommon in the Hamptons."

Your partner, Leonard Kramer had an accent too and so did Curtis.

"He was born in Holland. Curtis in Minsk."

And you?

"Osseo, Wisconsin. Norwegian territory."

DR. JOHNSTONE

Schweinbauer was one of two Nazis sentenced by the Russians for unspeakable war crimes.

What crimes? Jake wanted to know

The cremation of innocent men, women and children, many still alive when the fires burned, I said.

I heard years back. I was told I must never, never speak of this and then I could not speak at all..

Jake. you can speak now. I told him. You've come out of the darkness. Those fears, those ghosts are dead.

No. They are always there. My family name is not Swain. It's Schweinbauer!

In that moment I saw. I imagined what could have happened. Years back, Schweinbauer must have shown up at the Swain household in Delmarva, revealed the arrest by the Russians and then the Americans and then his release and then his presence and the sworn secret of silence.

He's my Uncle Hans. A murderer. Out there free all these years.

I didn't tell him about the Mossad. I did say David was looking for him and that he wants to bring him to Israel to stand trial.

Another trial, What for?

To show the world what he did.

Why not just kill him?

LYLE HUNTER

Jake and I were in our room. kind of sitting around. waiting to head to the ballpark. I noticed he didn't have his notebook. So, we wouldn't be talking. Well, I'd be talking and Jake listening.

I was telling how great things were looking with Norfolk close to going to the Triple A World Series against the El Paso Chihuahuas. EL Paso was running away in the Pacific Coast League and we had two series coming up against Durham Bulls, the Tampa Bay franchise, and the Syracuse Mets.

"If we beat the Bulls and the Mets we're going to the big game, the championship game. You excited as I am, Jake?"

He didn't answer.

"Come on! Nod! Write something."

"I can talk."

"Whaaat? No shit!? Wow!"

"Yeah, I'm back. Hope I don't go silent again."

"How great! Wait till the team finds out."

"Don't say anything, Lyle. I don't want them to know yet."

"Why not?"

"I may have to leave the team. Going to use the disability as an excuse."

"Leave where? Why? Did you knock up Dixie?" "Nobody's going knock her up. She's got all kinds of sprays, creams, and a diaphragm."

"You know I've got my eye on Essie Lang. She's got some ass on her."

I don't know how Jake and I got into this. I guess for me it was talking about anything but Jake leaving the team and not being here for the big series with Durham and Syracuse.

"I gotta find someone." Jake said.

"And you're gonna leave the team? You can't do that. It's Hunter and Swain and pray for rain, like the great time Spahn and Sain."

Jake hung his head.

"Please don't do it. Jake."

'We'll see."

"Fuck that. I'll never forgive you."

ERIC SWAIN

The kid came home on his day off. He never did that before and he didn't even call to say he was coming. Just popped in. I didn't know what to expect. The reports on him in the Norfolk papers were glowing. I hoped he came to give us the news that he was going up to the Major Leagues. He motioned me to the parlor. He didn't have his writing pad. So, he'd be repeating the last word I said. I asked him if he was okay.

"I'm back now," he said," I can speak."

"Holy shit!! God, that's great. How'd it happen?"

"Just happened. But it's not why I'm here."

I asked him if there was something wrong.

"We need to talk."

"Okay."

"Do you know where Uncle Hans is?"

"No, haven't heard from him in about 25 years or more.. And even back then he wouldn't tell me where he was living."

"Why were we all told not to speak of him or know of him?"

"Something to do with the War. I think he was on the run."

"From who?"

"The Jews. Maybe the Soviets. They said he was a war criminal."

"Like Adolf Eichmann or Hermann Goering or Julius Streicher?"

"I don't know."

"I went dumb after that visit by Uncle Hans. I would close my eyes and see you standing there with your index fingers crossed over your mouth."

"Hans wasn't as bad as those others."

"Many of the hundreds of Nazis sentenced to death killed themselves. But Uncle Hans ran and hid."

"He was trying to save his life."

"Where is he?"

"I don't know. He might be dead. He's eight years older than me."

"That would be best."

"Why are you saying that?"

"There is no end to remembering. There is no redemption from what the Nazis did except by killing them."

JAKE

Had to talk to David Essich. Find out what he knew about Uncle Hans. I knew when he had his appointment with Dr. Johnstone so I waited across the street at an out-door café till he came out. Lyle had tossed me a copy of the *Central-Islip News* when I left, saying there was a report of my triumph against the L.I. Ducks in there.

The paper compared me to the great Cardinal pitcher, Bob Gibson. I scanned the rest of the paper and started to read an account of a murder when David came out.

I walked over to him. He wrinkled his brow. He was puzzled, didn't know what to expect from a guy who couldn't talk. And when I said, "do you have a minute?"

"What? You've been fooling everyone, faking it? I understand neurotics but you're whacked out."

Recovered a fumble, I told him. Back in the ballgame, this time with a voice.

"I don't know whether to listen to you or run."

Please listen, David.

"Okay, but if you start acting nuts, I'm gone."

I told him I understood he was with the Wiesenthal group. ...

"Who told you that?"

Saw you on the History Channel in Mr. Wiesenthal's office.

"Shouldn't you be playing baseball?"

Day off.

"Day off and you want to spend it with me--?"

I'm looking for a former Nazi and so does your group. How do you find them?

"Let's sit down and get a coffee."

When his double expresso and my coke came, he told me. "It's complicated, mostly research, going through documents, like the many trial records of which Nuremberg trail is best known."

What do you look for?

"All sorts of things—those tried in absentia. Nazis that escaped, disappeared like Eichmann and Heinrich Muller. Muller was a high-ranking gestapo and a police official, central in the planning and execution of the holocaust."

And you work with our government in catching those that escaped?

"We try to enlist their help. And the help of other countries. Some cooperate, some don't."

The Israelis help, I heard that.

"If the Mossad doesn't get in the way."

What do you mean?

"If they find them, they kill them. We want to bring them to trial, tell the world what they did."

But in the end you'll kill them.

"Or let them rot in prison for the rest of their lives."

I don't understand. I told David. What's the point of a trial? I asked David the same question I asked Dr. Johnstone.

"So that humanity doesn't forget what they did. Tens of millions of people died in the six years of conflict and genocide. Reminders. Got to keep reminding. How many on your team have even heard of the Nazis?"

I knew many Nazis committed suicide which may have meant they understood --crime and punishment.

"Don't get into it, Jake. Leave it to us"

I don't know if I can.

"Why, you got a particular Nazi in mind?"

I decided not to tell him. Because I was thinking of killing Uncle Hans myself..

DET. GIL TOTTEN

The Curtis case was still nagging at me. Nobody knew who he was or where he came from. I tried war records, birth records in Long Island, New York, New Jersey, Connecticut. Zip. Then, I don't know why, I thought of my cousin Andy. He was a full sergeant in the military police, stationed at Dover Air Base in Delaware, the place they bring the dead soldiers.

Andy had earlier been stationed at the biggest hospital outside the US near Landstuhl, Germany. It was a long shot, but Andy knew things, knew people in Army Intelligence. I sent him Curtis' prints and the photo on his driver's license

More than a month past before Andy called.

"Gil, his name is not Curtis. It's Gerhard Oberhauser. Former SS brought to interrogation Center near Richmond, Virginia. He had been spying on the Russians for the Nazis and the Army wanted to pick his brain. He stayed in a minimum Army security prison for 18 months and was released."

No follow-up?

"Lost in the woodwork."

Was he brought to the US alone?

"I didn't look for that. But it stands to reason if there were other Russian experts captured we would have sent them to Richmond."

Thanks a mil, Andy. Say, you're in Delaware. When you get a break why don't you come here. Central Islip is not that far. We'll have a couple of laughs.

"Okay," he said and hung up without another word. That's Andy. Duty done.

Nazi connection? Ummm.

LYLE HUNTER

You're not going to believe it. I certainly couldn't and I've been knowing and watching Jake for longer than anybody seeing the game. We were in Durham, at the Bulls stadium. Jake took the mound for the seventh inning. For the previous six innings, the Durham Bulls looked pitifully sad, dejected, as they sat in their dugout. Jake was masterful, never saw him as dominant –pop-ups, pitiful grounders, so many swings and misses. It looked like he only had to take the mound and the Bulls might just as well stay silent at the plate, not even try to swing.

Jake came out for the seventh and final inning. And something happened. He could not find the plate. High, wide, low over the catcher's head. He walked the first three batters. We were only up by two runs. The pitching coach hurried to the mound.

"What wrong? You hurting, Jake? Pulled something?"

He shook his head.

The manager had sent me to warm up after Jake walked the second guy.

"Take a seat. You did great, Jake. We'll call Hunter."

From the bullpen, I saw the coach reach for the ball. But Jake wouldn't give it. The coach gesture was of an insistent man. Jake pointed to the bench. The coach stamped his foot. Jake turned him around and gave him a little shove. That's when the umpire came out to the mound. He barked a few words at Jake and the coach. Finally, the coach gave up.

Jake was back on the mound. His first three pitches were balls. Then he turned, picked up the rosin bag, slammed it down, took the hill, and threw six straight strikes, all timed at over 101.1 miles per hour on the speed gun, with the highest being 104.3. He'd never thrown a ball that fast before. He was faster than the great Walter Johnson and Bob Feller.

The clubhouse was elated. We'd taken the first step to the World Series. Jake was fined 7500 dollars and suspended for four days.

When I was alone with Jake I asked him what happened, He had walked batters before but never that wild and never more than two walks a whole game.

"I can't tell you."

"Because you don't know or won't tell me?"

"Because I was thinking about what it would take to kill someone."

"Are you going whacko?

I was worried about him, hoped he was still seeing that psychiatrist.

JAKE

Lyle is a great guy, a true friend. a buddy, a pal. How could I tell him I lost focus on the mound because I was thinking of Raskolnikov and how detective Porfiry and the prostitute Sonia urge him to submit only to God? If I find my uncle and kill him, is it a sin against God and not a human being, even if the human is deserving of death.

Listening in to Dr. Johnstone and Essich the Russians sentenced Uncle Hans to only five years in prison. That's a sentence they might give to white-collar criminal for bankruptcy fraud, or cooking the books. Or maybe a first time drug possession charge.

I had read 200 German war crime defendants were tried and sentenced to death in Nuremburg. And it was reported that another 1600 were tried, convicted and sentenced to death or long jail terms under traditional channels of justice. Some of these were killed in prison by other inmates.

And Uncle Hans slips through the cracks and is alive and well in the US. Fuck Raskilnikov had his mad sense of sin and God.

You are going down --if not the Russians, the Mossad than me.

DAVID ESSICH

I keep worrying about the Mossad getting to Schweinbauer with their noose before we can snatch him and take him to Israel to stand trial. The Mossad can be strangely inconsistent; it makes its own judgment. It was essential in the capture of Adolf Eichmann, the architect of the Holocaust who organized the sending of millions of Jews and others to the death camps. To the Mossad Eichmann was the personification of evil who had to be put on trial for the world to see the face of evil. Whereas in the case of Schweinbauer and Oberhauser and Otto Klemm, the other SS man, who was going under the name Kramer, the Mossad thought of them as vermin, cockroaches one just steps on. The Mossad saw them as little shit birds diligently interested in advancing their careers in the Nazi bureaucracy.

Maybe the Soviet judges who sentenced Heizrohr and Schweinbauer to only 5 years felt the same. I know Col. Pedrova saw them as amoral monsters deserving of the death penalty.

I'm hoping to put Schweinbauer on the stage and let the world see the bastard for who he is. And I can't say I'm not. worried about Jake Swain getting in the way.

DET. GIL TOTTEN

Who should walk into the station but Jake Swain? I got a call from the Desk Sergeant and I couldn't believe the kid was here, asking for me.

He was standing at my desk. I'd never seen him before. Up close, I mean. Good looking kid, about six feet, well proportioned, handsome face. I couldn't for the life of me imagine why he wanted to see me. And then I had heard that the kid couldn't talk.

You knocked the daylights out of us. The Ducks have been the top team in our league for three years running. I told him. And then...boom. The kid was speaking.

"Must have been the stars and moon were in the right place. Don't know what happened. Every pitch I tossed worked."

I was so surprised that he was talking, I was struck dumb for a bit.

All the reports I read said you couldn't speak.

"Couldn't for 12 years. And then I got my voice back."

Okay. I'm happy for you. What can I do for you?

"I read that you were on the murder of Alvin Curtis and that you had discovered something about the dead guy."

Yeah, but it's still an on-going investigation and I can't disclose anything. We're still looking for the killer. What's your interest in Curtis?

"I may have an idea who killed him."

Oh--?

"Tell me what you found out about him and if it jibes with what I heard, I'll tell who killed him."

Jake, it's illegal to withhold evidence or knowledge about the case.

"This is not about legal or illegal, Detective Totten. It's a swap."

The kid was a great pitcher but right then I thought he was a little whacky, You either ignore crazy people or you try to draw them out if you are still working a case.

I laughed. Okay, why do you think you know the killer? I asked him.

"Because I heard something about clean unexplained killings."

I asked him what he heard.

"That they are extremely professional and often carried out be spy agencies."

So you think the CIA or the KGB is involved?

"Not them."

Who?

"Your turn," he said.

What I tell you must not be told to anyone, nobody, not your family, friends. I mean NOBODY. It must not be brought up at any time.

Jake nodded.

Okay, Alvin Curtis was not his real name. His real name is Gerhard Oberhauser: he was a former SS man, captured, brought here served time and released.

"A Nazi."

I nodded.

"Then Your killer is the Mossad. I happen to know that the Israelis kill Nazis in hiding deemed not worthy to stand trial."

And how do you know that? I wanted to know.

"I saw it on the History Channel. And I checked and someone at the Wiesenthal Center told me it was true."

Okay, the Mossad's on the list of perpetrators, Jake.

I appreciate your coming in and remember, MUMS THE WORD. Can I ask you why you are so interested in Nazis?

"Because I have an Uncle who is an escaped Nazi hiding somewhere in this country."

The kid got more interesting by the minute.

When he left, I started thinking about Leonard Kramer in Riverhead and Aaron Jacobson in Water Mill, Critis's partners.

JAKE

I came to realize that if Curtis was SS so must have been the murdered partner in Riverhead and perhaps even the other partner in Water Mill. It wasn't hard to check the GE affiliates to find the name of the company and its owners. Was the Water Mill partner, Aaron Jacobson, SS? Or an innocent dupe the SS men attached to.

I was still on suspension for another two days so I caught a plane in Norfolk to La Guardia and rented a car to get to Water Mill. I found the mall and the business showroom easily enough, but didn't go right in. First, I stopped at Walmart went to the counter where they sold riffles, target pistols and hunting knives. The knife I liked came in a box and I asked the guy behind the counter to rap it.

"They'll do that for you at checkout." He told me.

So, I took the wrapped box and walked to the GE franchise.

Inside, a nice looking woman with a big smile asked if she could help. I told her I wanted to see Mr. Jacobson.

She asked why. And I told her it was something personal.

"Well, you see, there's been something unforeseen that has come up and it has upset the boss and he's not seeing anyone."

I told her I think he'll see me. "I'm family."

"Oh, wait here. I'll let Mr. Jacobson know."

I walked into Jacobson's office. He was standing near the door—a man in his 70's. about my height, crew-cut gray hair. He didn't bother to ask my name. Perhaps he knew it, and would know that my name was Swain like his was Jacobson.

Still, he asked, "Who are you?"

I can't say I recognized him as Uncle Hans. Perhaps he had plastic surgery. Something different around the eyes and chin.

"I'm a pitcher in triple A baseball. I played a game recently against the Long Island Ducks in Central Islip, Long Island, where your partner was killed.

"A bad day for the company. How'd you know he was my partner?"

"It was written up in the *Central-Islip News* on the day after I had pitched there."

"But you told my assistant you were family—"

"Well, you see, I had an Uncle who escaped from Germany during the war and went into hiding in this country."

His face, his expression didn't change except for a little movement of his of his jaw as if he was feeling his tooth with his tongue.

"Like many Germans, I guess," he said

You're not German? I asked.

"No. I'm Norwegian American from Osseo, Wisconsin."

I was beginning to have my doubts. Perhaps he wasn't Uncle Hans. I tried to remember if Uncle Hans had given his hiding name to my father. If he had I'd forgotten it. Of course, he could still be another SS, like Curtis and maybe Kramer.

"You know, Jacob, if you have an Uncle in hiding it is best not to go around looking him or talking to people about him, unless you want him to be caught."

I never gave my name. Jacobson was Uncle Hans. And soon I will kill him.

LYLE HUNTER

Jake's suspension was up and just in time, too. The game with the Syracuse Mets was this afternoon. The coaches were still pissed off with him and they told me I'd be going against the Mets. I was nervous. I'd faced them twice before during the year and we had lost both but I got two no decisions. The games were tied when I was relieved. But it was nice that Jake was here. It was a comfort to know he'd be in the bullpen, if I faulted.

When he walked in he was holding a box and when I asked him what was in it, he told me a hunting knife.

I never heard Jake talk about hunting so it was curious he'd buy a knife, especially one about 8 inches long. But with Jake you didn't ask many questions because you wouldn't get any answers for much of the time I knew him. Jake was private, mostly he read serious books about the War. I remember a couple that he read. One was more than a thousand pages called

The Rise and Fall of the Third Reich, and another *A Spy In the Heart of the Third Reich.* I used to wonder what was so fascinating about the Nazis. One of these days I'll ask him.

But now, it was the Syracuse Mets.

"Jake you think we'll beat the Mets?"

"I know we will. You faced them before."

"Yeah, two no decisions."

"Third time the charm," he said.

You know, Jake had a way saying something and you'd believe him.

Let's go the field.

"Hunter's ready."

I managed to get out of the first inning, not before they had scored on three straight singles.

When we came to bat, Jim Ramirez our first baseman, launched a bomb and the game was tied. It stayed that way till the fourth inning when the Mets blasted a couple of bombs off me and the score was 3-1 Mets. In the 7th inning, I found my groove and when we came to bat Craig Costello, our catcher, hit a homer with a man on and we were tied again. But in the 8th inning, I walked the first hitter and the next guy bunted and I slipped fielding it and there were two men on.

The manager came out to take the ball and he signaled for Jake to relieve me. But Jake didn't move from the bullpen. He waited for Jake about 25 seconds when one of the bench coaches came running out to the mound. He told the manager that Jake wants Hunter to finish and he won't relieve him.

"Cocksucker!" -- the manager.

Then the umpire came out and the manger told him "we're not making a change."

I was so proud and thankful to Jake who was now surely fucked with the team that I had a surge of energy and I found my groove with two scoreless innings and in the ninth we scored the winning run.

Jake was called in the manager's office and was refined 5000 bucks and suspended again. His fines of 7500 the first time and 5000 for today was about one third of his yearly salary.

I went up to him to thank him and offered to give him half my monthly salary for the rest of the season. All he said was "third time the charm."

I was almost in tears.

Later, I ran into the manager and he was still boiling. "That fucking Swain. He's crazier than all the nuts we had in baseball. And good fuckin riddance!!"

You're not firing him?

"Firing? No, the bastard's going up to the Majors. Let Baltimore worry about him."

How great!! Jake was going to the Majors. And all the fines they hit him with didn't matter now. A rookie in this first year makes 300 Grand.

And later I worried Jake seems to be self-destructing.: What's he going to do with that hunting knife?

EMILY SWAIN

It was in all the papers—*Baltimore Sun, Richmond Post-Dispatch even The New York Times*. My boy was a Major leaguer in what must have been record time. I loved it, but it didn't surprise me, really. Jacob was always special even as a baby. The first words of most babies is usually "Mama." Jacob's first words were "Hold me." Can you believe it?

He was much loved. When the girls played house, Jacob was the adored baby. As the first few years past, Jacob was showing us how smart he was. When we played guessing games Jacob knew more answers than a boy his age could have known. And sometimes more than his sisters. And then when he started school, the teachers told me he's very, very smart. They were thinking of skipping him, but decided not to do it because the other children would be bigger, older and it could bother a child emotionally.

I think the most special thing about Jacob was how aware he was. I can remember fighting with Erick –can't even remember what we fought about – but Jacob came to me and said, "If Daddy doesn't love you, I will not love him." Can you believe it? Jacob was always sensitive. I remember he was 3 years old and had enlarged tonsils and Erick took him to the hospital to have them removed. He settled him in the hospital nursery. And instead of waiting till they took him into surgery, Eric left. When he came home, Jacob wouldn't have anything to do with his father, wouldn't even look at him for a month. Our saddest days, of course, was when Jacob could no longer talk. But now, with his voice back his "Miraculous climb to the Major Leagues," as the *Baltimore Sun* put it, we are a blessed family. I don't mean to say we are perfect. We have our black marks, our dirty little secrets, Erick's brother Hans, a war crimes Nazi is hiding in the US. So different from Erick who wasn't even 17 years old and sent to fight in North Africa. By the grace of God, after the war he somehow fell into Eleanor Roosevelt's saving of war refugees and was brought to this country. That's the way Erick tells it. Let it be. I don't know if Erick was one the Hitler's youths. It seems he could have been. There are so many tangled, complex, twisted stories of escaped Nazi war criminals . Someone told me of a weird one she either saw on TV or in the movies. Grace

Hunter, Lyle's mother, is the couch potato or couch potatoes.

Two old Jews in a nursing home, one, Sam, with dementia who sits around remembering the death camps. The other, Nathan, who had been at the same concentration camp as Sam and who both seemingly suffered cruelties from that Nazi guard. I can't remember the guard's name-- maybe Otto Krause, Anyway, Nathan stirs Sam up to hunt for Otto Krause, who is hiding in America .Nathan gets the names of three Otto Krauses. and Sam escapes from the nursing home, buys a gun, and tracks the three Krauses in three different cities. One is dead. The other one was a Lutheran minister who was too young to be Krause. And the third one was a Rabbi. Then, Sam, having failed, comes back to the nursing home where it is revealed by Nathan that Sam is Krause and Nathan blows his brains out with Sam's gun. So, you see? Hidden Nazis…they can be anywhere. Turn around and you might find an Otto Krause. So goes the Swains. It's not even our real name. But who cares? In the melting pot everything is real.

JAKE

I'm in Baltimore now. It's a lot different from Norfolk, everything's bigger flashier, more crowds, dozens of reporters from NBC, WAR, WJZ, FOX NEWS and then the local papers. Everybody wants to talk to me and I've only been here a week. I haven't even pitched yet. The manager is a good guy or seems so now.

"Jake, I heard about your shenanigans in Norfolk. You might have gotten away with that in the minors but it's not going to work here."

That was special, sir. During most of my time in Norfolk you never heard a peep out of me.

"That was because you couldn't talk."

Okay, I said. I didn't want to explain further.

"What number were you wearing down there?"

32, I told him.

"32, eh? Good thing you're not with the Dodgers. That's spoken for. That's Sandy Koufax's number."

If I'd known that I would have refused. I told him.

"Refused, why?"

It wouldn't seem right.

"What number do you want?"

I shrugged.

"We'll give you 44"

"Jake Swain is with the big club, wearing number 44, and it can't be said it's a lucky number because Jake Swain has been a 'lucky' pitcher where ever he went. And the charm continues here in Baltimore . He was called in to relieve in a meaningless game against the White Sox with Baltimore leading 8-0 and promptly struck out the side. Welcome to Baltimore, Jake Swain!! The article was written by Don Felder of the *Sun*.

All the papers are glowing about me. The manager asked me who my agent was and I told him I don't have an agent.

"You'll probably have one soon because the Tonight Show called. Johnny Carson wants to talk to you."

I didn't want to talk to him. Actually, I didn't want any publicity. I wished I couldn't talk again. I was studying the best way to kill Uncle Hans.

GIL TOTTEN

Maybe the kid was on to something and that the Mossad took out the escaped SS men. I wasn't going to catch them. That's international doings and I doubt if the Feds cared. Maybe MI 5 or MI 6 would investigate but we're not Great Britain.

Then there's Aaron Jacobson in Water Mill. He's in trouble if the Mossad has him targeted. I don't know if he's a Nazi in hiding, but I could take a shot at getting his prints and photo and passing them to my cousin Andy. Most jurisdictions like to keep a tight hold on their murder cases. Riverhead gave me a hard time in finding out about Kramer and I suspect the Southampton police to be the same about one its citizens. I got a camera, drove to Water Mill, and sat on a bench outside T J Maxx, the store facing Jacobson's operation.

I was there more than two hours starting at 7:00 am and no Jacobson. I guess he wasn't coming to work. A guy approached and asked what I was doing there. He told me he was security for the mall. Showed me a badge.

We're in the same business, I said. And I told him that he was interfering in a murder investigation, showed him my shield. He stepped back, turned and left. And I waited to no avail.

JAKE

It was easy to find Uncle Hans' address in Southampton. It was listed in the telephone book. We had a night game with the Yankees in the Bronx and I took off at 6:00 in the morning, rented a car from a dirt cheap rental company off the Grand Concourse and headed for Southampton. I got to Uncle Hans house about an hour later and waited. When he came out and started walking to his car, I caught him from behind and had the knife at his throat. I took his gun, led him to the trunk of my junkbox and as I struggled trying to get him into the trunk, the knife cut his forearm, not deep, but it was bleeding some. I heard his dogs barking and growling but they were nowhere in sight.

The New York Public Library, according to the Times, was showing a gruesome, horrifying display of Holocaust photos on its second floor and I wanted to see Uncle Hans face as he looked at them.

An hour later I dumped the car on 41st Street and kept the knife at his back while we walked through Bryant Park and around to the side entrance on 42nd Street.

Something odd happened; he wasn't resisting any more.

He loosened up and just walked with me through the entrance and up the marble stairway to the exhibit room.

I still kept the knife pointed at his ribs. For an exhibit on the Holocaust in New York you'd expect it to be crowded but there were only four others and they seemed to be leaving. It was after 3:00 and maybe the other viewers had gone back to work.

As we went from one photo to the next – one more horrifying than the other, pictures of skeletal men, women, and children with hollow eyes being shoved into furnaces, the ones he built and had watched as they had burned. The caption said, *Lebensunwertes Leben* --Llves unworthy of Life. The next few showed what seemed like hundreds of starving people locked in with dead bodies.

Uncle Hans didn't speak, but looked down at the blood on his hands. I stopped at every photo for at least 3 minutes for him to fully take in the horrors—a pile of gold wedding bands and teeth yanked from Jews' jaws, a huge collection of shoes one or two with feet still inside. Perhaps the victims were too slow getting them off, and a concentration camp guard with a baby on his bayonet.

Let's go, I said.

"Go where?"

To hell.

And I covered his mouth and slit his throat. He was dead when he crumbled to the floor. I had to get to Yankee Stadium. We had played two high-scoring, long games and I wasn't used much and had to be on hand.

You probably read it in the papers:

MURDER IN THE LIBRARY

And if you turned to the back of the paper you couldn't miss another headline:

ROOKIE PITCHER SHUTS OUT THE YANKEES.

Maybe Detective Totten will figure it out one day and when he comes for me, I'll go silent again.

THE END

9 781649 453754